LOTTIE LUNA

AND THE BLOOM GARDEN

VIVIAN FRENCH

Illustrated by Nathan Reed

HarperCollins *Children's Books*

For the real Lottie,

with much love

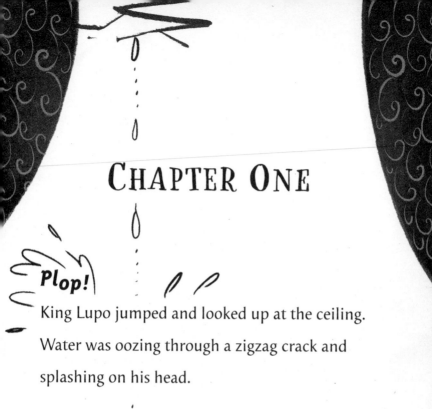

CHAPTER ONE

Plop!

King Lupo jumped and looked up at the ceiling.
Water was oozing through a zigzag crack and
splashing on his head.

'I did warn you, dear,' said Queen Mila. 'If you will insist on sitting at the head of the table, you'll get dripped on.' She passed the king a napkin and he wiped his ears.

'A king should always be kingly,' he announced. 'I may not have been king for long, but I do know how to behave. A king is head of his people, so he should sit at the head of the table – drips or no drips! And talking about behaving, 'WHERE is Lottie? She's late for breakfast!'

'I think she's getting ready,' Queen Mila told him. 'Do remember, dear – it's her first day at her new school, so she's bound to be a little nervous.'

'Nervous? Why would she be nervous?' King Lupo dodged another drip and took a bite of his toast. Finding it was soggy, he made a face and put it back on his plate.

Queen Mila sighed. 'You know how happy she was at her last school, dear. She had lots of friends and was popular with the teachers too. She doesn't know anyone at Shadow Academy. She's starting all over again.'

'But she's the daughter of a king now!' Lupo raised his whiskery eyebrows. 'She'll find that she's treated with the greatest respect!'

'I don't think—' Queen Mila had been about to say that she didn't think that would make any difference, but she was interrupted by the door being flung open with a crash, and Lottie appeared. She was clutching her school bag in one hand and a bunch of pencils in the other, which she waved wildly at her mother.

'Ma! I can't find my pencil sharpener anywhere. It's hopeless! Ever since we moved, everything's been upside down. Nothing's where it should be – *and* there are ZILLIONS of spiders in the bathroom! Do we have to live here?'

Boris, Lottie's older brother, stopped admiring himself in the cracked old mirror by the fireplace and joined in. 'But we're royalty now, Lottie! Pa's a king, and kings live in castles – even if they are a bit crumbly and falling down.'

'Well said, Boris my lad!' King Lupo beamed at his son. 'Dracon Castle is our home. I'm sure once we've done a few repairs we'll be extremely comfortable here. Now, Lottie, sit down and eat your breakfast.'

'Hmmmph . . .' Lottie sighed thoughtfully as she remembered her old home. Although it had been small and cramped, it had been warm and very cosy. The castle they had inherited had so many rooms she couldn't count them all, and every single one was freezing cold.

'I'm not hungry,' she said. 'Honestly, Pa,

I couldn't eat a thing.' She looked at her mother. 'Ma – do you think it'll be okay at Shadow Academy? It's awful being new in the middle of a term.'

Her mother hugged her. 'I'm sure you'll make lots of friends in no time at all.'

'Huh!' Boris looked down his nose. 'Who'd want to be friends with her? Not me!'

Lottie made a face at him, then stuffed her blunt pencils into her bag. 'I'll be off now,' she said. 'I don't want to be late, not on my first day. See you later, darling Ma. Remember I won't be back until after moonrise! Bye, Pa!' And she whisked out of the dining hall, banging the door behind her. Jaws, her pet bat, was waiting for her on the other side, and together they hurried along the cold, dark corridor. With a heave and a tug, Lottie managed to open the creaking front door . . . and then they were out in the morning sunshine.

As Lottie ran down the long, winding path that led from Dracon Castle to the village below, she was already worrying about the day ahead. 'It's all very well Ma saying I'll make friends, Jaws, but what if I don't? They'll probably hate me because Pa's the new king, and they'll think I'm all posh and stuck-up when I'm not. But . . .' An idea popped into her head, and she stopped to think about it. 'What if I don't tell anyone I live in a castle? Or that Pa's a king? I'll say I'm plain Lottie Luna and that I'm really rather ordinary, just like everyone else.'

Liking the idea, she walked slowly on. 'But what about my superpowers? Can I hide them too?' She touched the little moonstone necklace that she always wore and then, with a decisive nod, tucked it under her jumper. 'There! It's gone.' And with a skip and a jump she was on her way.

If anyone had watched Lottie running along, they would have easily guessed that she wasn't the ordinary little werewolf she so badly wanted to be. Born on the night of a lunar eclipse, when the moon was full, she had been gifted with special powers. She could run like the wind, her eyesight was as sharp as an eagle's, and she was far stronger than her older brother . . . She had other, less obvious, powers too.

The little moonstone necklace she had been given on the day she was born reflected her moods. Now, as she ran, it was glowing pure white beneath her jumper. Jaws, flying above her head, was aware of it, and that made him happy too. He looped a loop, then swooped down to ride on Lottie's shoulder.

Twenty minutes later, Lottie and Jaws reached the gates of Shadow Academy.

'Oh, dear . . .' Lottie was wide-eyed as she looked at the huge grey stone building in front of her. 'I do hope it's going to be all right. What do you think, Jaws?'

Jaws fluttered round her head. '*Eeeek,*' he squeaked. '*Eeeek!*'

'You're right.' Lottie took a firmer hold of her school bag. 'I'm Lottie Luna and I'm not scared of anything!' And with her head held high, she marched up the steps and in through the wide-open front door.

CHAPTER TWO

A tall boy was waiting in the hallway of Shadow Academy. When he saw Lottie, he gave her a little wave. 'Are you Lottie Luna? I've been waiting for you. I'm Wilf, and you're in my form. I'm going to show you around.'

He caught sight of Jaws, and his eyes shone. 'Hey! Is that your bat? Does he always come to school with you?'

'Should I have left him at home?' Lottie was worried, but Wilf grinned at her.

'It's fine. Pets are welcome. I've got a pet rat myself.'

'Oh, good.' Lottie smiled back. 'They were allowed at my old school – just as long as they didn't squeak too much during lessons.' She stroked Jaws's furry head. 'He's usually very good.'

'My rat's terribly badly behaved,' Wilf said cheerfully. 'He crept into Mrs Wilkolak's cupboard last week, and knocked all the paint pots over, so now he's banned.' He giggled.

'You should have seen the mess!'

Lottie wasn't sure whether to laugh or not. 'Did you get into loads of trouble?'

Wilf shrugged. 'Not too much.' He gave her a sideways look. 'Don't worry. It's okay here. You'll get used to it really quickly. We're really all right.' Wilf paused for a moment. 'Well, except for Awful Aggie.'

It was Lottie's turn to giggle. 'Awful Aggie? Who's she?'

'Agatha Claws –' Wilf crossed his eyes – 'she thinks she's the best at everything!' He paused for a moment and scratched his head. 'And then there's Bruno – Bruno Gnawbone. He's a bit of a mystery.'

'How is he a mystery?' Lottie was interested.

Wilf shrugged. 'His dad's the deputy head teacher. They were both new this term, and none of us can make them out. Bruno doesn't talk much, but he's always listening in, and we're sure he tells his dad everything. Don't tell him any secrets!'

'I won't,' Lottie promised, and Wilf grinned at her.

'Good! Now, it's this way. Our classroom's right at the end of the corridor.'

As Lottie followed Wilf, she whispered to Jaws, 'He's nice. I like him!'

There were pictures and notices on the walls and she looked at them with interest. Some of the pictures were of famous past pupils, and others showed exciting-looking moonlit trips and events.

There seemed to be a lot of things going on – a forest club, a group that met to do moon dancing, a star-gazing club . . .

'I'll join all of those,' she decided.

There was also a large notice about a competition. Lottie wanted to stop and read it, but Wilf was hurrying her along too quickly. She only had time to see that it was something about a special garden. *Interesting*, she thought. *I'll definitely have a look at that later.*

'Here we are,' Wilf said at last, pulling open a door and giving a mock bow. 'Please enter!'

'Thank you,' Lottie said. She could see rows of faces looking at her, and for a moment her stomach was full of butterflies. *Don't be silly, Lottie Luna*, she told herself, *they can't eat you!* And she took a deep breath and walked in.

The teacher, an elderly werewolf with greying fur and little gold spectacles, greeted her warmly. 'Hello, Lottie! Welcome to Shadow Academy! I'm your teacher, Mrs Wilkolak, and I hope you'll be very happy here.'

'Thank you,' Lottie said. 'Ummm . . . where should I sit?'

'Perhaps you'd like to take the empty seat next

to Aggie?' Mrs Wilkolak suggested.

'That's me!' A very neat and tidy girl with a long nose gave Lottie a cool smile. 'So you're Lottie . . . Is that your real name? It's a bit boring. My name's Agatha Astra Claws. Astra means star, you know.'

Lottie saw Wilf rolling his eyes, and she smiled at him. He winked back, and a girl on the other side of Lottie stifled a giggle.

Aggie took no notice. 'So where do you live, Lottie?' I live in the new house up on the hill, near that awful Dracon Castle. My father says it should be pulled down. He says it's an eyesore!'

Jaws, sitting on Lottie's shoulder, gave a protesting squeak. Lottie, making sure no one could see her, put her finger to her lips to silence him.

'Thank you, Aggie.' Mrs Wilkolak's tone was firm. 'That's quite enough.' She turned back to Lottie. 'Now, Lottie, I should let you know about a competition that's running here at school at the moment – a competition to transform the wasteland at the back of the academy.'

Aha! Lottie thought. *So that's what the notice in the corridor was about!*

'This land has been allowed to grow wild,' Mrs Wilkolak went on. 'A businessman wants to buy it, but the owner says that if we can make it beautiful she'll give it to us instead. It would be wonderful to have that extra bit of space at the back of the school. So every pupil is going to draw their dream design, and the head teacher, Mrs Grubeloff, is going to choose the best one. Do you like gardens and flowers?'

Lottie nodded enthusiastically. 'Yes, I do! I had my own garden at our last house, and I loved it! Ma and I arranged little white pebbles all round the edge, and they shone white in the moonlight . . .'

A wave of homesickness for her old house suddenly swept over her, and she stopped.

Mrs Wilkolak gave her a sympathetic look. 'That sounds delightful. Why don't you take a piece of paper from my table and see what you can do.'

As Lottie sat back down at her table, Aggie smiled a superior kind of smile. 'I don't expect *you* know much about gardens, but *I* do. We've got three gardeners, and we grow simply marvellous flowers.'

A small boy with strange green eyes leaned forward from the table behind. 'Aggie's sure to win,' he said. 'She's very clever.'

Aggie nodded. 'I am.'

Lottie wasn't sure what to say, but the girl who had giggled earlier gave a loud sigh. 'You don't need to tell us, Aggie!'

'Actually, Marjory, I was trying to be helpful to Lottie,' Aggie said, 'and so was Bruno.' She gave the boy with green eyes a little nod. 'Weren't you, Bruno?'

Bruno didn't answer, but Lottie thought he looked pleased. She remembered the name from earlier – so this was the deputy head's son.

Mrs Wilkolak clapped her hands. 'Class W! If all you're going to do is chat, we'll never find a winner for the competition. I'd like you to work for another thirty minutes, and then we'll go outside and show Lottie the garden and the lake.'

A lake? Lottie's eyes shone, and she put her

29

hand up. 'Please, Mrs Wilkolak – can we swim? Is it allowed?'

'We do allow swimming on hot days,' Mrs Wilkolak told her, 'but you have to be careful. The lake's small, but it's very deep. Can you swim, Lottie?'

'I absolutely LOVE swimming!' Lottie beamed at her, and Jaws squeaked in agreement. 'I was—' She stopped dead as she remembered she'd decided to be ordinary Lottie Luna. At her last school she'd been the year's swimming champion. She'd have to remember to swim slowly. *And splash a lot*, she told herself. All the same, she was thrilled, and as she picked up her pencil case she was smiling happily.

CHAPTER THREE

It was only when she saw her pencils that Lottie remembered how blunt they were – and she didn't have a sharpener. She turned to Aggie and asked if she had one that she could borrow, but Aggie shook her head.

'I never lend my sharpener,' she said. 'It might get spoiled. It was VERY expensive.'

'Here, use mine,' someone said, and the same girl as before – Marjory – leaned across to pass it over, and Lottie thanked her.

I like her, Lottie thought to herself, *and I expect*

I'll get used to Aggie . . . Well, maybe. And she settled down to plan her dream garden.

It seemed no time at all before Mrs Wilkolak was clapping her hands and asking everyone to put their plans on her table. 'Well done, all of you,' she said. 'I hope you enjoyed yourselves!'

'I've designed an utterly beautiful garden,' Aggie announced. 'All the roses will be pink, the paths will be pink, and there will even be little sparkly pink lemonade fountains everywhere.'

'Yuck!' Wilf spoke more loudly than he'd meant to, and Aggie glared at him.

'Just because you haven't got any good ideas,' she said, 'you don't need to be rude!'

Mrs Wilkolak nodded. 'That's quite right. I don't like rudeness in this classroom. Wilf – apologise to Aggie at once, please!'

As Wilf was making a half-hearted apology, Lottie noticed there was a faint smell of peppermints in the classroom, and she saw Bruno was chewing. Without thinking, she said, 'Ooh, so we're allowed to eat sweets – how lovely!'

Mrs Wilkolak was shocked. 'Eat sweets? Certainly not! Whatever made you think that, Lottie?'

Too late, Lottie remembered that her special powers gave her a much keener sense of smell

than other people's. She could feel Bruno's furious glare on the back of her neck as she stammered, 'No, I just – I was just wondering, that's all.'

But Mrs Wilkolak was suspicious. She got up from her table, and it was obvious that she was about to investigate further.

'Oh, no!' Lottie held her breath, but—

RRRRRING!!

The bell went and the teacher changed direction.

Phew! Lottie thought as Mrs Wilkolak told the class to line up.

'Time to go out to the garden,' Mrs Wilkolak said. 'Make sure you wipe your shoes when you come back in!'

Lottie followed Wilf and Marjory, and found

Bruno right behind her.

'Just you wait, you sneak!' he hissed. 'I'll get my own back, you'll see!'

Lottie spun round. 'Fine, I'll be waiting!' she said, then she bit her tongue. When would she ever learn to think before she spoke?

Once outside, Lottie looked around her in delight. The lake was sparkling in the sunshine and there were several cherry trees in amongst the long grass and thistles. They were old and twisted, but they were covered in snow-white blossom. 'That white blossom will be so beautiful in the moonlight,' Lottie whispered to Jaws, who fluttered close to her. 'And my plan is for a moonlight garden—'

Her thoughts were interrupted by Aggie, who was looking at the trees and frowning. 'Those are horrible,' she said. 'They're so ugly! If I win, I'll have them cut down. They won't be in MY garden!'

'Squeak!' Jaws had landed on Lottie's shoulder and was waving a wing. Lottie turned to look where he was pointing, and saw a teacher leading a group of tiny werewolf cubs out from the school. Each of them was carrying a piece of paper and a crayon, but the littlest one was skipping in circles, and not looking where he was going. 'Be careful!' the teacher warned. 'Stay near me. Don't go too near the lake!' But just as she turned back round again, the smallest cub dropped his piece of paper. The wind caught it and blew it towards the shining water, and

the little cub dashed after it. He slipped – he was
in the water and sinking fast.

'Help!' he screamed. 'Help! I can't swim!'

Lottie began to run. She ran like the wind,
forgetting about everything except saving the
tiny cub. As she came close to where he had
disappeared, she dived into the water – a long,
smooth dive without a single splash.

There was no sign of the cub now, except for a few bubbles. Down Lottie swam, down and down. Where was he? All she could see was water weed. She looked again . . . and there he was!

She grabbed him and headed for the surface. The next moment, she was swimming back towards the side of the lake, the whimpering cub in her arms. She climbed out, dripping wet, and gave him a hug. 'Don't cry any more,' she said comfortingly. 'You're safe now.'

As she put him on the ground, she was astonished to hear applause: her classmates, Mrs Wilkolak, and the tiny cubs and their teacher were all clapping. 'Hurrah for Lottie!' Wilf shouted, and there was a loud cheer.

Lottie blushed and shook her head. 'It was nothing,' she said.

'Well done, Lottie!' Mrs Wilkolak smiled warmly at her. 'You're an amazingly fast swimmer! It was quick thinking too. Now hurry inside and get dry. And our head teacher will certainly want to thank you when I tell her what you did today – although I suspect she'll have seen what happened through her window. She sees most things.'

'Oh!' Lottie looked anxious. 'Will she be cross with me?'

'Of course not!' Mrs Wilkolak said. 'Now, Wilf and Marjory – could you take Lottie to the home room? There are towels there, and some spare clothes. Hopefully there'll be something to fit you. We keep clothes mainly for the little ones . . . they're always getting themselves covered in paint and mess.'

As Wilf, Marjory and Lottie walked away, Lottie heard Aggie mutter, 'What a show-off. Did you see her, Bruno? Diving straight in without asking anyone first.'

Lottie couldn't hear Bruno's answer, but she

42

was sure he was agreeing with Aggie, and she sighed. Sometimes having extra-special hearing was a problem: you heard things you weren't meant to hear.

Wilf saw her expression. 'Cheer up,' he said. 'You're a hero, Lottie Luna! I'm really glad you've come to Shadow Academy!'

CHAPTER FOUR

Lottie could feel butterflies in her stomach as she walked down the corridor to the head teacher's office. She was wearing the strangest collection of clothes and didn't feel at all comfortable. Aggie, who was supposed to be showing her the way, had sneered at her too-tight jumper and too-large trousers before pointing at a staircase. 'Up there, then straight on. You can't miss it. Not unless you're *really* stupid, of course.'

Lottie was sure she *could* miss it, but didn't say anything in case Aggie made another unpleasant

remark. She headed up the stairs and looked carefully at each door on the corridor until Jaws, who was circling above her, pointed with a claw.

'Up at the end?' Lottie asked him. 'Thank you, Jaws.'

The end door had a small brass plaque on it: 'Madam Grubeloff. Knock and wait!'

'Be brave, Lottie Luna!' Lottie told herself, and she knocked as firmly as she could.

'Come!' The voice was brisk, and Lottie could feel Jaws trembling on her shoulder as she walked in . . . and gasped.

Madam Grubeloff's office was not at all how Lottie had imagined it would be. It was light and airy, and the walls were covered with drawings done by her pupils. A huge window looked out on the lake and overgrown wasteland, and

45

plants tumbled happily over the window
ledge. Books were piled untidily against the
walls, and a comfortable sofa was covered with
heaps of cushions and soft woolly throws.

Madam Grubeloff herself was quite young, with pale grey fur and big brown eyes. She jumped up from her desk, ran towards Lottie and shook her hand so enthusiastically that it made Lottie smile. 'So you're our heroine! Well, Lottie Luna – I can't tell you how delighted I am that you've joined us here at Shadow Academy! You saved little Bernie – such a naughty little cub! He has seven much older brothers and I'm afraid he's just a little bit spoiled. I'm so very, *very* grateful to you.'

Lottie blushed and a warm glow spread up from her toes. 'Thank you!' she said, and then something caught her eye. Madam Grubeloff was wearing a moonstone necklace . . . a necklace very like her own. Lottie's heart skipped a beat; Jaws quivered.

'Please, Madam Grubeloff . . . may I show you something?' And she pulled out her own necklace.

'You were born when there was a full moon and a lunar eclipse,' said Madam Grubeloff.

She sounded as if it was the most ordinary thing in the world. 'As soon as I saw you running, I knew.' She suddenly looked serious. 'Your powers are a gift, Lottie – they make you special. But they will bring great responsibility, and may sometimes be a problem too.'

Lottie sighed. 'I just want to be plain Lottie Luna, not someone special.'

The head teacher looked at her thoughtfully. 'I see. And am I right in thinking you don't want your friends to know that you live in Dracon Castle, or that your father's a king?'

Lottie blushed again. 'People make such an awful fuss about kings and queens and princesses and stuff like that,' she said. 'I'd much rather be ordinary.' She leaned forward. 'Can I ask you a question, Madam Grubeloff – about the powers?

50

Sometimes I hear things I'm not meant to hear . . . What should I do when that happens?'

Madam Grubeloff threw back her head and roared with laughter. 'Oh, Lottie! You and I will have to have a little secret! Everybody wonders how I know the things I know . . . but I'm like you – I can hear pupils and teachers talking from the other end of the corridor. Sometimes I can even hear what's going on inside a classroom when the door is closed!' Madam Grubeloff stopped laughing. 'But we, with our special powers, must always respect people's privacy. The only time we should make an exception is if we hear something that might endanger others. It'll be up to you to decide what you should hear – and what you shouldn't.'

Lottie nodded. 'I'll try my best.'

'Good! Now, hurry back to class, and please give this note to Mrs Wilkolak. I want to have this evening's Howl a little earlier than usual.' The head teacher suddenly looked questioningly at Lottie. 'Did you have an Evening Howl at your last school?'

'Oh, yes.' Lottie nodded. 'We always all got together at the end of the day to sing at moonrise, unless it was summertime.'

'It's just the same here,' Madam Grubeloff told her, and she handed Lottie a piece of paper and patted her arm. 'Thank you again, Lottie Luna.'

As Lottie made her way back down the long corridor, she gave a little skip of happiness. 'Hey, Jaws, I didn't need to worry! I'm going to love being here! I've already got two new friends, and Madam Grubeloff is AMAZING! And I'm sure

Awful Aggie and Bruno will be okay too. After all, what can they do?' And Lottie gave another little skip.

Jaws didn't answer. He was pleased to see Lottie so happy and her moonstone necklace glowing pure white, but he had his own opinions about Aggie and Bruno.

CHAPTER FIVE

Mrs Wilkolak nodded when she read the head teacher's note. 'Evening Howl will be early tonight,' she announced. 'Madam Grubeloff is going to announce the winner of the garden competition.'

Aggie sat up, looking very pleased with herself. 'That'll be me!' She gave Lottie a superior smile. 'I win everything, you see. My father says I'm very, very special.'

Wilf growled something under his breath, but Aggie just stuck her nose in the air. 'Some people

are just SO jealous!' she said. 'I can't help being clever. It just comes naturally.'

The rest of the day went very quickly. Lottie found, much to her relief, that she could remember the names of most of the stars in the astronomy lesson, and after astronomy they had moon studies.

'I've written a WONDERFUL poem about the moon,' Aggie announced, and she read it out. Lottie was surprised to find it was very good, and she joined in the clapping at the end with enthusiasm.

'That was excellent, Aggie,' Mrs Wilkolak said, and Aggie bowed, pink with pleasure.

She does love being best, Lottie thought to herself.

The last bell went soon after. There was just

enough time to tidy the classroom and get ready for the Evening Howl. Lottie was sent to change back into her own clothes, which were now dry. When she got back, she found to her disappointment that the class had already started leaving the classroom. Wilf and Marjory were nowhere to be seen, so she had to follow behind Aggie and Bruno.

Quickly, they walked down corridor after corridor and into the Great Hall. Lottie gasped. She had never seen anything quite like it. The ceiling was painted with swirling clouds and silver stars, with walls of midnight blue. There were no windows, and the hall was lit entirely by tiny sparkly lights. Soft music was playing, and Lottie was sure she could hear the distant sound of owls hooting. 'It's beautiful!' she breathed.

Aggie sounded almost friendly as she said, 'It is, isn't it?' Then she gave a self-conscious little cough. 'Actually, my grandfather built it.'

'Wow! He was really, *really* clever!' Lottie was so obviously impressed that Aggie smiled at her.

'My dad's a builder too,' she said. 'And so is Bruno's dad.'

'No he's not!' Bruno was scowling. 'He's a teacher!'

'Oh, yes.' Aggie was flustered. 'I forgot. He's a teacher now, but he used to be a builder.'

Lottie wasn't sure what to say in answer, but at that moment Madam Grubeloff sailed on to the stage, and everyone was silent. She was wearing a long black cloak trimmed with silver, which made her look much grander than she did when Lottie met her earlier. The music stopped, and she

58

looked around. 'Good evening, everyone.'

There was an answering chorus of, 'Good evening, Madam Grubeloff.'

'Before we have our Howl,' the head teacher said, 'I have an important announcement to make.'

At once there was a rustling and whispering, and Madam Grubeloff held up her hand for silence. 'As you know, you were all asked to design a garden for the wasteland behind the school. The owner has said that she will let us have it if we can make it truly beautiful, and you have all been working hard to create a very special place where we can feel peaceful and at ease, walking among flowers, looking at the water—'

'I did fall splosh in the water, though!' a squeaky voice interrupted.

'Thank you, Bernie. So you did.' Madam Grubeloff smiled at the tiny cub. 'And before my announcement, I'd like to thank one of our pupils, a pupil who not only joined us today, but did a very brave thing too.' Lottie felt herself begin to blush and she stared hard at her feet. 'She saved little Bernie from drowning,' Madam Grubeloff went on. 'Thank you, Lottie. Not only that, but she has also designed a delightful garden. It therefore gives me great pleasure to declare that our competition winner is . . . Lottie Luna! Lottie, would you please come and collect your certificate of honour?'

Wilf and Marjory led the applause as Lottie made her way up on to the stage. Only two people didn't join in – Aggie, who stood open-mouthed, and Bruno.

As Lottie took the certificate, Madam Grubeloff

smiled at her. 'Well done, Lottie!'

Lottie smiled back. 'Thank you most enormously,'

she said. 'And could we . . .' She hesitated,

in case she was about to ask too much, but

Madam Grubeloff looked at her encouragingly.

'Yes? What is it, Lottie?'

'Could we possibly call it the Bloom Garden? I've chosen flowers that look extra beautiful in the moonlight . . . Would that be all right?'

'Oh, *yes!*' The head teacher clapped her hands. 'That would be PERFECT. It would make our full-moon parties and ceremonies extra special. I love that idea!'

It seemed that everyone else loved the idea as well. The applause grew even louder as Lottie made her way down from the stage, but as she passed Bruno he sneered at her. 'You only won because you can swim,' he hissed. 'Your garden's rubbish! Aggie's was much better.'

Lottie was saved from replying by the sound of an owl hooting three times, and the hall fell silent.

'The time has come to join together,' Madam Grubeloff said. 'Everyone – take your neighbour's hand.'

Aggie didn't look at all happy as she held out her hand to Lottie, but Lottie gave her a friendly grin. 'What happens now?' she whispered.

'Look up,' Aggie said, and Lottie glanced up at the beautifully painted ceiling. Slowly, very slowly, a silver moon floated out from behind the swirling clouds. Lottie held her breath as it shone brighter and brighter, almost as if it was real.

WOW! she thought, when at that moment Madam Grubeloff began the Howl. It started very low, gradually building to a wonderful harmony

as all the teachers and pupils joined her. Lottie

could feel the hairs on the back of her neck

prickling as the noise grew louder and louder.

At her last school, the Howl had been nothing

special, but now she felt as if she was swept up

into something so grand and magnificent that her heart swelled with pride.

I'm so very glad we moved, she told herself as the Howl gradually died away and Aggie let go of her hand. *Goodness! I've SUCH a lot to tell Ma and Pa!*

CHAPTER SIX

The next day, Lottie woke up early and, much to her mother's surprise, bounced down to breakfast before King Lupo had even started on his boiled egg.

'Lottie!' Queen Mila said. 'What's happened to you?'

'I can't wait to go to school!' Lottie told her. 'I want to meet up with my new friends so we can make a start on my Bloom

Garden. I had such a lovely day yesterday!'

'I hope they treated you with the right and proper respect, Lottie. Remember, you're a princess now!' King Lupo sliced the top off his egg. 'Oh, it's runny! I do hate runny eggs.'

Lottie shook her head at him. 'Don't go on and on about that princess stuff, Pa. I'm fine.' And she grabbed a piece of toast and headed for the door. Jaws, who was dozing on the curtain rail, woke with a jump and flapped after her.

As soon as she reached Shadow Academy, Lottie ran round to the wasteland. She was delighted to see that there were already signs of action. There was a large board pinned on the fence with a rota on it, and two young werewolf pupils were already pulling up thistles and weeds. An older werewolf in a suit was standing watching, but when Lottie wished him a cheerful 'Good morning!' he frowned at her.

'And what exactly do you think you're doing here?'

Lottie stared at him in surprise. She had seen him before, at the Evening Howl, and had wondered who he was. He'd been looking cross then, as if he wasn't enjoying it.

'Excuse me,' she said politely. 'I'm Lottie Luna . . . I designed the garden. I've come to help.'

'And I'm Mr Gnawbone, the deputy head of Shadow Academy. I'd have thought a clever little werewolf like you would have known that. Aren't you supposed to be the best at everything, Lottie Luna?'

As the older werewolf sneered at her, Lottie noticed that he had the same strange green eyes as his son, Bruno. He was still sneering as he added, 'It's no good trying your goody-goody tricks on me. You should be in school, not wandering about where people are trying to work. Your name isn't on the rota until later. Don't let me see you here again unless you're with your teacher.'

'But . . . but . . .' Lottie wanted to remind him that it was her garden design that had been chosen for the wasteland, but she didn't want to sound rude. Jaws, hovering above her, saw her moonstone necklace turn dull, and knew she was upset. Flying down, he settled on her shoulder to comfort her.

'Do you understand?' Mr Gnawbone growled. His eyes were very cold.

'Yes, Mr Gnawbone,' Lottie said, and she hurried back inside the school.

68

As she walked down the corridor to her classroom, with the little bat still on her shoulder, she wondered why Bruno's father had been so mean to her. *Maybe Bruno told him that I nearly got him into trouble for eating mints*, she thought.

'Hi, Lottie!' It was Marjory. 'Have you been to look at the garden?'

'Yes, but Bruno's father told me off for being there on my own,' Lottie said, and Marjory pulled a face.

'He's horribly strict. He's new, so we're all hoping he won't last here for long. No one likes him – he's not a bit like the other teachers.'

Lottie didn't like Mr Gnawbone either, but she decided not to let that spoil her day. 'What lessons have we got today?' she asked.

Marjory looked vague. 'Night shadows, I

think . . . sort of mixed up with working out distances. We're doing a study on night running and how long it takes to get to different places. Hey! You can run really fast, can't you? We saw you yesterday. You were mega-speedy.'

'Only because Bernie was in trouble,' Lottie said.

Marjory gave her a sideways look. 'I don't want to pry, but is there something special about you,

Lottie? You can run like the wind, and I've never seen anyone swim as fast as you did.'

'Mmmm . . .' Lottie blushed. She was tempted to explain, but she did so want to be just like everyone else.

'It's okay,' Marjory said quickly. 'I shouldn't have asked.' She squeezed Lottie's hand, and Lottie gave her a grateful smile.

'It's nothing. Truly. And I'm terrible at geography – you'll have to help me with that.'

Wilf was already in the classroom when Marjory and Lottie walked in, and he jumped up when he saw them. 'We're not going to have proper lessons today,' he told them. 'Isn't it brilliant? We're all going to help to create the Bloom

Garden instead! Apparently, the owner wants to see how it turns out as soon as possible, so she can decide whether she wants us to have the land – or whether she should sell it to the builder. He wants to put a road through to Dracon Hill.'

'He wants to build a road?' Lottie asked. 'A road at the back of Shadow Academy? That's horrible!'

Just then, Aggie came into the classroom. She heard what Lottie said and sniffed. 'SOME builders are very nice,' she said. 'My father certainly is.'

'Sorry, Aggie.' Lottie was genuinely apologetic. 'I'm sure he is.' She looked at Bruno, who was beside Aggie as usual. 'I met your father just now, Bruno. He looks much more like a teacher than a builder, doesn't he?'

74

Bruno went bright red with anger. 'What do you mean? My dad IS a teacher! He's never been a builder. Never!'

'But Aggie said—' Lottie stopped. Aggie was glaring at her. 'Sorry . . . I must have got that wrong.'

'Yes, you must have,' Bruno growled. 'Completely wrong.'

Lottie was still trying to think of something to say to put it right, when Mrs Wilkolak came hurrying in and she was saved from answering.

'Time to get ready, everyone,' their teacher said. 'We've lots to do today!' And five minutes later, the whole class was outside.

'This is better than geography,' Marjory said, as she pulled up a large thistle. 'Can we help every day, Mrs Wilkolak?'

Mrs Wilkolak chuckled. 'I'm sure you can help again tomorrow morning – *if* you promise to work extra hard tomorrow afternoon!'

'We promise!' Wilf, Marjory and Lottie all spoke together, and Mrs Wilkolak chuckled again.

'It's a deal!' she said.

By the end of the day, the garden was looking very different. All the weeds had been cleared, and a large area had been dug over, ready for planting. Lottie had marked out the pattern for her design with white pebbles. Mrs Wilkolak had promised to make sure there would be enough to edge the paths. 'And plenty of white flowers,' Lottie said dreamily. 'Lilies and moon daisies – I love those! – and

night-scented stocks . . .
and orange blossom,
and lots and lots of
Queen Anne's
lace . . .'

Marjory looked at her in wonder. 'How do you know so much about flowers, Lottie?'

'We had a garden where I lived before, and Ma and I both love flowers.' Lottie giggled. 'My poor pa's hopeless, though. He can't tell a daisy from a dandelion!'

'Does your new house have a garden?' Wilf asked.

Lottie came down to earth with a bump. She had to be careful – she could see Aggie was listening, and she really didn't want her to find out that she lived in Dracon Castle. She hesitated, then said, 'We do, but it's a bit wild at the moment. I don't think anyone's bothered about it for ages.'

But Aggie had seen her hesitation, and her gaze sharpened. 'So where exactly do you live, Lottie?'

'Oh . . . up on the hill . . .' Lottie waved a vague

hand and tried to change the subject. 'I forgot to say, we ought to have roses. Little white ones, as well as pink and red. And at least two benches, so people can sit and rest . . . and maybe lilac too – lilac smells absolutely lovely in the evening.'

Aggie started to say something about roses but was interrupted by Mrs Wilkolak. 'Everyone, inside. It's nearly time for the Evening Howl, and you all need a good wash first.'

As Lottie jumped up, she wondered if perhaps it was time to tell Wilf and Marjory about Dracon Castle. *After all, they're my friends . . . I don't want to keep secrets from them.* And the thought made her happy as she hurried off to wash her hands.

CHAPTER SEVEN

On Wednesday morning, Lottie woke up early again. She skipped down to the kitchen, and found she was the first; even her mother wasn't up yet. She put the kettle on and, as it boiled, her brother Boris appeared, yawning.

'Good,' he said. 'You can make me my breakfast.'

'Make it yourself,' Lottie told him.

'I've got to get to school!'

Boris looked at her curiously. 'You really like that place, don't you?'

Lottie's eyes shone. 'I do! It's wonderful! They're all lovely . . . Well, not Aggie and Bruno, but everyone else is.'

'What's wrong with Aggie and Bruno?' Boris raised a hairy eyebrow.

'They're just a bit mean, that's all.' Lottie didn't want to explain.

Boris frowned. 'You're a princess, Lottie. Nobody should be mean to a princess.'

Lottie shrugged. 'I don't see why not,' she said. She didn't want to tell him that nobody at school *knew* she was a princess. 'I'm exactly the same as I was before we came here and we became royalty. Look, do you want some toast, or not?'

Her brother growled, but all the same he helped himself to the toast that Lottie had made.

'Oi, you didn't say thank you,' she reminded him, but he just growled again. Lottie sighed and ate her toast at record speed.

Five minutes later, she was racing Jaws down the hill. As she reached Shadow Academy, she saw Wilf standing outside and she waved to him. 'Hi!' she called. 'You're early too! Do you think we could go and look at the garden? Mr Gnawbone said I shouldn't go there on my own, but I really want to see—' Lottie stopped as she realised Wilf was looking unusually serious. 'What is it? Are you okay?'

'It's the garden,' Wilf said. 'Someone tried to

wreck it last night. Come and have a look.' And he took Lottie's hand and led her round the back of the school.

'OH!' Lottie could hardly believe her eyes. 'Oh, no!' All her white pebbles had been picked up and thrown into a pile, and one of the beautiful cherry trees had been attacked: broken branches lay on the ground, the white blossom like fresh snow. The newly dug area was now covered in litter, and bits of broken glass gleamed in the sunshine. 'This is terrible!' Lottie said, and there were tears in her eyes. 'We haven't planted a single flower yet and it's already been destroyed. Who could have done it?'

Wilf shrugged. 'I don't know, but we mustn't let them beat us! We'll clear it again, Lottie. We've got to have our Bloom Garden!'

'Well said, Wilf.' Madam Grubeloff had seen them from her office window and was coming out to join them. 'We've never had anything like this happen before. I'm shocked! But you're right. We won't let them beat us.' She turned to Lottie. 'You're looking very thoughtful, Lottie Luna. What's on your mind?'

Lottie blinked. 'I'm not sure,' she said, but she wasn't being entirely truthful. She was remembering how Aggie had said she hated the old cherry trees, and how she'd chop them down if it was her garden. Could Aggie have had anything to do with it? Maybe she would talk to Wilf and Marjory about it later, but she didn't want to mention it now.

'Oh my goodness gracious me!' Mrs Wilkolak had come hurrying out. 'And after all your hard work too! What a shame . . . Who on earth would want to spoil a garden made by children?'

'Someone who doesn't want it to be a garden,' Wilf said. 'You can count on us, though, Lottie Luna. We won't let them beat us. The Bloom Garden's going to happen!'

The garden was cleared once again. By the time school ended, Lottie felt much happier. She had spent the rest of the morning wondering if she should tell Wilf and Marjory her suspicions about Aggie being behind the destruction of the garden. But what if she was wrong and Aggie hadn't done anything at all? Wouldn't Wilf and

Marjory think she was being mean for even thinking such a thing?

When Mrs Wilkolak announced that the flowers were due to arrive the next afternoon, excitement made Lottie put her suspicions to one side. Even better, Mrs Wilkolak promised Lottie, Wilf and Marjory that they could help with the planting. 'Just as long as you work really hard in the morning,' she said, but there was a twinkle in her eye and Lottie was sure there wouldn't be a problem.

At once, Aggie put up her hand. 'That's not fair,' she protested, and several other children nodded. 'Why will *they* get to go out and do planting, and we won't?'

'We could get it planted much quicker if everybody helps.' Lottie looked hopefully at their teacher, and as she spoke she remembered her suspicions again. If everyone helped plant the flowers, she'd be able to keep an eye on Aggie without anyone else noticing. 'Don't you think it would be so much nicer if we all worked on the garden together, Mrs Wilkolak? That would really make it Class W's Bloom Garden!'

Mrs Wilkolak pretended to sigh. 'My goodness, Lottie Luna! What a demanding girl you are! But you're right. Yes, you can all help tomorrow . . . IF you work hard in the morning!'

That evening, Lottie skipped home, while Jaws flew happy circles above her. 'Tomorrow's going

to be a wonderful day,' she told him. 'Once the flowers are planted, everyone will be able to see what a lovely garden it's going to be. I'm sure it won't take too long, Jaws, not now everyone's going to help.' Then a thought came to her, and her eyes shone. 'Maybe we could even have a special moonlit celebration once it's finished. It'll look even prettier then . . . Oh! I can't wait!'

CHAPTER EIGHT

On Thursday, her fourth day at Shadow
Academy, Lottie was even earlier. The school was
very quiet, and there were no signs of life. She
paused at the main door and listened, but she
couldn't hear a thing. As she tiptoed round the
side of the building, she took a deep breath . . .

The next minute she was staring, her heart
beating so fast that her chest hurt. The garden!
Today it was in even more of a mess than the day
before. Piles of broken bricks were dumped where
the flowerbeds were supposed to be, the white

pebbles had been thrown aside in a heap, dirty cardboard boxes and old rags were scattered all around, and bits of paper fluttered in the breeze.

'Oh! It's ruined,' she whispered. 'It can't ever be a garden now. Oh, who could be doing this?' The thought that it might be Aggie crossed her mind again, and she looked anxiously at the cherry trees. There didn't seem to be any more damage to them. She was about to go and check when a voice stopped her.

'WHAT are YOU doing, Lottie Luna?' It was Mr Gnawbone. He was loping towards her and glaring angrily. Lottie didn't want him to see her face because she had been trying so hard not to burst into tears, so she bent down to pick up a piece of paper. 'I told you yesterday, you shouldn't be here on your own,' he went on, 'but it seems you want to disobey me. One more mistake and you'll be in serious trouble!' And with that he stormed away, growling as he went.

Lottie hardly heard what he was saying, though. She was staring at the wreckage of the garden, seeing the end of all her hopes and dreams. 'It's too much for anyone to clear up,' she said quietly. 'They're sure to build the road here now.' And, with a sob, she turned and started walking slowly back towards the school.

'Lottie!' Marjory was running towards her. 'What is it?' When she reached Lottie, she put her arms round her and hugged her. 'What's happened?'

'It's the garden,' Lottie said miserably. 'It's been wrecked again.'

'WHAT?' Marjory's eyes were like saucers, and Lottie nodded.

'There are bricks and rubbish and mess everywhere. I think it must be my fault somehow. Everyone says that nothing like this has ever happened before . . .'

Marjory shook her head. 'It's NOT your fault. Some horrible person is behind this.'

93

Lottie rubbed her eyes and made up her mind to tell her friend. 'Oh, Marjory, I can't help wondering if it might be Aggie . . .'

'Aggie?' Marjory looked puzzled. 'Aggie can be really mean,' she said thoughtfully, 'but I don't think she'd do anything like this. No, I think it's someone who wants to build the road, and that's why they're ruining the garden. Even if it had been Aggie's awful pink garden, I bet that exactly the same thing would have happened.'

This time it was Lottie's turn to stare. 'Are you sure?'

Marjory nodded. 'I'm not very clever, but I do think a lot. And I'm absolutely super-certain-sure.'

'WOW!' A huge smile spread across Lottie's face. 'You're the best friend ever, Marjory. You

94

really are!' Her eyes began to shine. 'So what we have to do is find out who wants to build this road. Ruining the garden is cheating – surely the owner won't want to sell the land to a cheat!'

'You're right,' Marjory agreed. 'Let's tell Wilf.'

Ting-a-ling-a-ling-a-LING!!!

Lottie jumped. 'What's that?' she asked.

'That's the Thursday assembly bell,' Marjory said. 'We'd better hurry. Madam Grubeloff doesn't come in on Thursdays, so Mr Gnawbone takes assembly instead – and he gets mad if anyone's late!'

And they dashed inside.

CHAPTER NINE

The Thursday assembly had a very different feeling from the Evening Howl. Mr Gnawbone began by telling everyone to sit up straight and pay attention. A couple of the very small wolf cubs were giggling, and he snapped at them so sharply they began to cry.

'Out!' Mr Gnawbone ordered. 'Out! Go and stand in the corridor until you've learned to behave yourselves!' And with that, the two little wolf cubs crept away.

'He's horrid,' Lottie whispered, and Wilf put his finger to his lips.

'**Shhh!**' he hissed.

But Mr Gnawbone had heard them. He peered down from the stage, his eyes gleaming. 'Who spoke?'

Lottie put up her hand. 'It was me. I'm sorry.'

'Aha! If it isn't our very own hero!' Mr Gnawbone jeered. 'So you think you're too special to obey the school rules, do you? Well, Lottie Luna, if you're hoping to stay here for any length of time, you must learn to do as you're told!'

Lottie could feel her cheeks flaming as she looked up at him on the stage. 'Yes, Mr Gnawbone.'

95

'And now I have an announcement to make.' Mr Gnawbone allowed himself a cold smile. 'As you may know, the wasteland at the back of the school has suffered a second attack by vandals. Madam Grubeloff is bringing the owner here tomorrow to see how things are progressing, but all she will see is bricks and rubbish. That being the case, she will undoubtedly make the sensible decision and sell the land so that a road can be built at the back of the school – a road that will provide easy access to Dracon Hill and the Forest of Murk.'

Sensible decision? Lottie looked up in astonishment. Why would the deputy head teacher not want the school to have a garden? It seemed really strange.

But Mr Gnawbone was still speaking. 'I have

stopped the order for the plants and flowers. The Bloom Garden is cancelled.'

There was a horrified intake of breath from almost everyone at Mr Gnawbone's final words, and Lottie clenched her fists. As she did so, she realised she was still holding the piece of paper that she'd picked up in the garden, and she gave it a quick glance.

It was a torn bill, dated from the week before. The name was missing, but the slogan caught her eye.

Come to us for all your building requirements.
Roadworks are our speciality!

Quietly, Lottie nudged Marjory and handed

her the paper. Marjory read it, only just managing to stop herself from gasping. Then – silently – she passed it to Wilf, who looked at it and mouthed, '*WOW!*'

'And WHAT are you looking at, Wilf and Marjory? Kindly bring whatever it is up here!' Mr Gnawbone was looking dangerously angry.

Wilf gulped as he began to make his way towards the stage. When he reached the end of the row, he sneezed and pulled a red spotty handkerchief out of his pocket. 'Sorry!' he apologised. 'I think I've got a bit of a cold.' He climbed slowly up the steps, hesitated as if he was nervous, then handed over the paper.

Lottie held her breath as the deputy head read it, but all he said was, 'I completely fail to see why this shopping list is suddenly of such interest. This is no way to behave in assembly. Go back to your place. And now –' he continued, turning back to the assembled school – 'we'll sing the Forest Song . . .'

When the dark night sky is pierced with stars
And the wind whispers secrets to the trees . . .

As the voices rose and fell in the old werewolf anthem, Lottie risked a sideways glance at Wilf. He was looking extremely pleased with himself and when he caught Lottie's eye he winked. *What did he do?* she wondered, but she had to wait until they were walking back to class find out.

'WOW! How did you do that?'

Wilf giggled. 'An old trick,' he said. 'I swapped the bill you found for my grandma's shopping list, when I pretended to sneeze.'

'You were BRILLIANT!' Lottie said.

'Just lucky I had Gran's list in my pocket,' Wilf said modestly.

Marjory was looking thoughtful. 'So why do you think that bill was in the garden?'

'I don't know,' Wilf said. 'It must have been in among the bricks and rubbish.'

A horrified expression came over Marjory's face. 'Hang on . . . Aggie's father's a builder, isn't he?' she said slowly. 'What if she got the bricks from home? And the rubbish – and that bill was mixed up among the papers?'

'Yes.' Lottie nodded. 'It's what I've been

wondering too, although I tried hard not to.' Her moonstone necklace was gleaming pale green as she rubbed her nose. 'Do you really think Aggie could hate me that much?'

Wilf and Marjory looked at each other. 'Yes,' they said together.

'Oh –' Lottie's stomach lurched at the idea that anyone could be so jealous – 'that's awful.' She was very quiet as they walked on down the corridor. It was only when they reached their classroom door that she suddenly spun round, her eyes sparkling.

'I've just had the most AMAZING idea! We CAN save the Bloom Garden! Can you stay on after school today, for a couple of hours? Mr Gnawbone might have cancelled the flower order, but we can clear a little patch and plant our own.

At least that will show the owner tomorrow what it could be like!'

'Just the three of us?' Marjory asked, staring at her. 'But there are LOADS of bricks! And all that rubbish . . .'

'And we don't have ANY plants,' Wilf added.

Lottie held out her hands to them. 'Please! I'm sure we can do it. I can shift those bricks. I'm . . . I'm really strong. And we can get some plants.

I'm . . . I'm . . . Look, I'll tell you exactly what I mean tonight – I promise!'

Wilf and Marjory looked at each other, then nodded. 'Yes, we'll stay,' Wilf said.

'Friends stick together,' Marjory agreed. 'But now we'd better get into class. We're late already!'

CHAPTER TEN

Mrs Wilkolak was not at all pleased when Wilf, Marjory and Lottie walked in late, even though Lottie apologised profusely and said it was all her fault. 'I still don't know my way round the school,' she said, hoping that this was near enough to the truth to not actually be a fib.

Mrs Wilkolak made a harrumphing noise. 'I'm beginning to wonder if you three are getting rather too pleased with yourselves,' she said. 'I do hope this bad behaviour isn't going to continue.'

Lottie shook her head. 'Oh, it won't, Mrs Wilkolak. I promise!'

As Lottie sat down, Aggie gave her a superior smile. 'I knew you weren't a real hero. I've NEVER been late!' Lottie didn't answer.

Mrs Wilkolak, who was still looking cross, set the class a comprehension test. She wrote on the whiteboard in capital letters:

SHAPESHIFTING
ENDURANCE
LONGEVITY

Then she frowned at the class over the top of her little gold spectacles. 'I want at least twenty words explaining each of these skills,' she snapped.

'So we get punished because Lottie's stupid enough to get lost,' Bruno hissed.

'I don't mind,' Aggie said smugly. 'I always come top at comprehension.'

The rest of the day seemed to drag. Lottie's idea was bubbling in her head . . . but would she be able to make it work? Would she be able to get the bricks moved and enough flowers planted in time to make a difference? She knew her special powers made her extra strong, but she'd still need Wilf and Marjory's help to clear away the rubbish.

Even the Evening Howl didn't seem as wonderful as usual that afternoon. Madam Grubeloff was still away, and Mr Gnawbone

rushed through it, and didn't even ask them to hold hands.

At long last the final bell rang, the school day was over and the other pupils gradually left the building. As silence fell, Wilf, Marjory and Lottie crept out from the woodshed where they'd been hiding since the end of school.

'So tell us, Lottie,' Wilf said as they hurried round to the garden. 'How exactly are we going to get these bricks moved? What's your secret?'

'Well . . .' Lottie took a deep breath. As she told them how she had been born when it was both a full moon and a lunar eclipse, and how it had given her special powers, including super-strength, Wilf and Marjory listened intently. As she finished Lottie added, 'But I don't want to be treated any differently. I'm exactly the same as everyone else! Truly!'

Marjory nodded. 'We're all the same but different. Like I'm good at geography, and Wilf's good at swapping bits of paper!'

'Exactly,' Lottie said, and then she hesitated. 'There's one more thing, though . . . We moved here because some old uncle of ours died, and Pa found he was a king. And Ma's a queen – although she's very bad at remembering it.'

'*The* king and queen?' Marjory's eyes opened very wide. 'Wow!'

'So that makes you a princess . . .' Wilf whistled softly.

Lottie wriggled with embarrassment. 'Sort of.'

Marjory smiled at her. 'It won't make any difference to us. I did wonder, just a bit, when you said you lived up on the hill. Dracon Castle's the only house up there, except for Aggie's.'

'I'm so glad I told you.' Lottie was feeling hugely relieved. 'And now – shall we get started on the garden?'

'Hey!' Wilf pointed. 'Over there – it's an old wheelbarrow! That'll help.'

Lottie ran to collect it and, when she came back, she was grinning. 'We've found another clue,' she said. 'It's not a school wheelbarrow – look!'

Marjory squinted at the faded letters. 'I can see an A and a W . . . and – yes! – it has the same slogan as on the bill: "Roadworks are our speciality!"'

'A . . . W . . .' Wilf said slowly. 'Maybe it once said "Claws"?'

Lottie stared at the letters. 'Claws . . . that's Aggie's name, and Aggie's dad's a builder!'

'So it has to be Aggie who's spoiling everything,' Marjory said. 'I'd say this proves it.'

'I think we should show it to Madam Grubeloff tomorrow.' Wilf was looking serious.

'Yes, we will,' Lottie agreed, 'but in the meantime—' She stopped mid-sentence. '*Shh*, someone's crying!'

Wilf and Marjory stared at her. 'I can't hear anything,' Wilf said. 'Are you sure?'

'It's coming from the school,' Lottie told him. She put her head on one side and listened again. 'Yes!' And then she was running, running like the wind. Marjory and Wilf looked at each other, then hurried after her.

It was hard for Lottie to find where the crying was coming from, as it stopped as soon as she rattled the outer doors to the school. At first, she couldn't find a way in, but an open window gave her the chance, and soon she was wriggling into a

classroom. Once inside, she ran up and down the corridors, calling, 'Hello? Where are you?'

'In here!' The voice was a squeak, and it was followed by a loud wail. 'I want my mummy!'

Lottie looked to the left and right, but all she could see was the large cupboard where the caretaker kept his mops and buckets. She pulled it open, and there inside was Bernie, the little cub she'd rescued from the lake. He was curled up in a ball and tears were trickling down his nose.

'Bernie!' she said gently, and she picked him up. 'Whatever are you doing in here?'

'I was hiding,' he said, 'but nobody came to find me. I want my mummy!'

Lottie kissed the top of his little furry head. 'It's all right. We'll take you home.' She tried hard not to think of all the work they needed to do in the Bloom Garden. 'Where do you live?'

'Round the hill.' Bernie wrapped his arms round Lottie's neck. 'It's a long, long way. Will you carry me? I'm ever so, ever so tired.'

Wilf and Marjory were waiting anxiously outside as Lottie lifted the little cub out through the window, then scrambled after him.

'Bernie got shut in a cupboard,' she explained. 'We'll have to take him home.'

'But what about the garden?' Wilf asked, and

115

Lottie heaved a massive sigh.

'We'll have to leave it. Bernie wants me to carry him . . . and I'm not sure I'll be able to find my way back here without you two.'

'But . . .' Wilf and Marjory looked at each other, then at the little cub, then back at Lottie. She was right. They needed to get the little cub home.

'We'll come,' Marjory said. Wilf nodded, and the little party set off.

In no time at all Bernie was asleep in Lottie's arms. She sighed again as she looked down at him. There was a painful ache in her chest, and from time to time she had to blink back tears as she thought about the little garden left behind at school. Marjory and Wilf walked silently beside her, while Jaws circled anxiously above. He

116

could see that Lottie's moonstone necklace was a gloomy purple, but he couldn't think of a way to cheer her up.

Bernie was right. It was a long way to his house, and even Lottie was feeling tired when she heard an anxious voice calling, 'Bernie! Bernie, where are you? Bernie!'

Bernie woke up with a loud squeak of joy. He jumped out of Lottie's arms, and ran towards the voice; Lottie, Wilf and Marjory ran after him.

'Bernie?' An enormous mother werewolf came hurrying towards them. 'Oh, you naughty, naughty little cub! I came to collect you from school, but you weren't there, so I thought you must have tried to come home on your own. I've been looking for you everywhere. I've been so worried.'

'I was hiding,' Bernie told her, 'but the door shut and it was dark and I cried and cried, but then Lottie found me and she bringed me home!'

Bernie's mother beamed at Lottie. 'That's so kind! I can't thank you enough.' Then a thought must have come to her, as her smile grew even wider. 'Oh! Are you Lottie Luna, the Lottie who saved Bernie from drowning? You're already our hero!'

Bernie tugged at his mother's arm. 'Mummy, Mummy! Lottie and Wilf and Marjory are making a garden!'

'Hush, Bernie, I know.' His mother nodded. 'Gurt and Loris told me.' When Lottie looked surprised, she explained, 'All my werewolves are gardeners – well, not Bernie, of course, but my older cubs – Gurt and Loris. They had an order to deliver a whole load of plants and flowers to the school today –' she looked puzzled – 'but then the order was cancelled, without any explanation . . . Do you know why?'

'It was because the garden was spoiled,' Lottie said sadly.

'Someone threw bricks everywhere, and rubbish, and made a horrible mess,' Marjory added.

'What?' Bernie's mother was horrified. 'Who would do such a mean thing?'

'We don't know.' Lottie sighed. 'We've already cleared it up once, but then they came and did it again.'

Bernie's mother's face lit up. 'But that's something *we* can do for you, Lottie Luna. We can thank you for saving Bernie by helping you make your garden! I'll send the boys up next week.'

Lottie's heart leaped, then sank again. 'Thank you, but I'm afraid that'll be too late. The Bloom Garden has to be ready for tomorrow, you see. That's when the owner's coming to look at it.'

'Ready for tomorrow? Then that's not a problem either. The plants and flowers that were ordered for the garden will still be on the cart.' Bernie's mother turned and bellowed up the

path, 'Boys! Come here! I want you – RIGHT NOW! There'll be no supper until Miss Lottie Luna's Bloom Garden is finished! Do you hear me? Right now, this minute!'

CHAPTER ELEVEN

Bernie's seven brothers, led by Gurt and Loris, worked as if their lives depended on it. In no time at all, the remaining bricks and rubbish were gone, and Lottie, eyes shining, was running to and fro, telling them where the plants were to go. Wilf and Marjory carefully edged the paths with gleaming white pebbles, and every so often the three of them smiled delightedly at one another.

'It's already looking beautiful,' Lottie said as the evening wore on. 'I can't believe how lovely it is!'

'It's absolutely gorgeous,' Marjory agreed. 'And it's very nearly finished.'

Wilf stood up and stretched. 'Do you think we should keep guard tonight?'

Marjory looked at Lottie. 'What do you think?' she asked.

'Maybe we should.' Lottie rubbed her nose thoughtfully. 'I couldn't bear it if it got spoiled again. But Ma and Pa'll worry if I don't come home . . .'

'I've got an idea,' Marjory said. 'Why don't you send Jaws home to tell your parents we've got an overnight project?'

'Brilliant!' Lottie beamed at her. 'Jaws, off you go!'

'And I'll run and tell Gran,' Wilf said. 'I'll be back in half an hour at the latest!'

'Can you tell my mum as well?' Marjory asked him. 'You'll be going right past my door.'

124

Wilf grinned. 'Sure thing.'

The gardeners were just putting the final touches
to the garden as Wilf came puffing back carrying a
bag of buns and apples and cake. 'Gran's the best,'
he said proudly. 'We can have a picnic while we
watch!'

'Oh!' Lottie said. 'That's wonderful!' And as
Bernie's brothers waved goodbye and hurried
home to have their supper, she settled down
on a bench with her friends to eat their picnic.
Above them the moon sailed up into the
cloudless sky, and the white flowers and cherry
blossom glimmered. As Lottie sighed happily,
and bit into an apple, her moonstone necklace
shone brightly . . .

'Oh!'

Lottie woke with a start. For a moment, she couldn't think where she was; above her was cherry blossom, and behind the blossom the sky was a pale blue. Was it the morning? Looking round, she saw that she was snuggled up on a garden bench; Marjory was fast asleep on one side of her, and Wilf on the other.

What woke me? she thought, and she turned her head this way and that, listening.

Voices! She could hear voices . . . and they were coming towards the garden. Silently, she woke Marjory and Wilf. 'Shhh!' she warned. 'Listen!'

'Well, hurry up and find it! How could you have been so silly? It's got our name on it! What were you thinking of? I told you to wreck the garden, not leave our stuff all over the place!'

Lottie, Marjory and Wilf looked at each other. Was it Aggie? Silently, they stood up and looked towards the corner of the school.

'Shhh!' Lottie whispered again. 'Here she comes!'

But it wasn't Aggie. It was Bruno who came hurrying round the corner with . . . his father! Mr Gnawbone, the deputy head!

Lottie stepped forward. 'Is this what you're looking for?' she asked, and she pointed to the wheelbarrow.

As Bruno and his father both froze, she went on. 'The letters A W are from Gnawbone, aren't they? It all makes sense now. First there was the piece of paper in among the rubbish . . . and then there was the wheelbarrow . . . and you were a builder before you were a teacher. We thought

127

that the A and the W were from "Claws" – Agatha Claws – but we should have guessed it was you and Bruno.'

Mr Gnawbone pulled himself together and sneered. 'Oh, dearie, dearie me!' he said. 'Perhaps you and your friends aren't so clever after all!'

'We're clever enough to catch you!' Lottie said fiercely.

'But not quite clever enough!' said Mr Gnawbone, as he drew himself up to his full height and glared down at her. 'Do you really think anyone's going to believe three silly young wolf cubs like you? I went to a lot of trouble to get myself into this horrible school as a teacher. I had to write my own references, and pretend I liked nasty little wolf cubs, and join in that ridiculous Evening Howl every night. I'm not

going to be beaten at the last minute! I'm going
to buy that land and I'm going to build that
road – and everyone who uses it will have to pay
me money! I'll make my fortune, and Bruno and I
will be RICH!'

'I'm afraid that's where you're wrong, Mr Gnawbone.'

There was a touch of cold steel in the voice, and Lottie held her breath as she saw Madam Grubeloff sweep towards them from behind a clump of trees.

'Did you really believe that I would allow a dreadful road to ruin our school?' the head teacher went on. 'I've had my suspicions ever since you came here – the way you treated the pupils, your ignorance of school traditions, the fact that you never joined in the Evening Howl . . . but you were clever enough to lie low for quite a while. Now, however, your plans have been uncovered – and I'm certain that when the owner hears about them she will want to give the garden to us.'

130

Madam Grubeloff flung out her arms. 'Just look! This is the most magical Bloom Garden ever!'

CHAPTER TWELVE

Later that day, when a very tired Lottie, Wilf and Marjory were back in class, Mrs Wilkolak announced that Madam Grubeloff had spoken to the owner, who had agreed they could hold the Evening Howl in the Bloom Garden on the following Friday. 'Wear your best clothes,' Mrs Wilkolak said. 'It's going to be a very special evening!'

'Wow!' Lottie had stars in her eyes when she looked at her friends. 'I can't wait! Won't it be amazing!'

Aggie looked down her nose at Lottie. 'What if it rains?'

'It won't,' Lottie said firmly, and then she added, 'I do hope you'll like the garden, Aggie. I put in lots of pink roses, just for you.'

'Oh!' An astonished smile spread over Aggie's face. 'Thank you, Lottie. That was . . . that was nice of you. And . . .' It was obvious Aggie felt awkward about something and was making a huge effort. 'And . . . I'm so very, very sorry that Bruno tried to spoil it.'

Lottie stared at her. 'Did you know it was Bruno?'

'Ummmm . . .' Aggie looked very uncomfortable. 'I kind of guessed it was. I knew Mr Gnawbone

had been a builder, because he'd worked with my dad, so it all seemed to add up. I didn't know Mr Gnawbone wanted to build a road, though. I thought Bruno was just doing it to get his own back on you.'

Lottie couldn't answer. She was feeling confused. Why hadn't Aggie said something earlier? But, then again, she'd been wrong to suspect Aggie . . .

She gave Aggie a huge smile. 'Don't worry about it,' she said.

The next week seemed to go very slowly. Lottie, Wilf and Marjory were counting down the hours, and they found it difficult to concentrate on their work. They did their best, however, and

Mrs Wilkolak was very patient.

There was no sign of Bruno, or his father. Wilf said that his gran, who worked in the bone store, had heard they had left home in a hurry with no forwarding address. 'Gone for good, Gran says –' Wilf grinned – 'and she's always right.'

At long last it was Friday. The day dawned bright and clear, and all the pupils arrived at school, laughing and chattering. Instead of lessons, Mrs Wilkolak showed the class how to make paper lanterns. As twilight fell, Class W trooped out to the Bloom Garden to join the other pupils and to hang twinkling lights on all the trees. Just as they hung the last lantern, Madam Grubeloff came sweeping out of the school in her long black cloak trimmed with silver. Beside her was an elderly werewolf who

walked with the aid of a stick. Lottie looked at her with interest. Was this the garden's owner?

Madam Grubeloff saw Lottie's interested gaze and smiled. 'Lottie, everyone – may I introduce Madam Talon de Scrazziola, the owner of the Bloom Garden! And Madam de Scrazziola, I believe you have something you wish to say?'

'Indeed I do.' The elderly werewolf nodded. 'I am delighted to be here . . . and I am even more delighted to see this very beautiful garden. It exceeds all my expectations, and I know it will bring you all joy for many, many years to come.' She opened her handbag and pulled out a scroll tied with a silver ribbon. 'This document states that from henceforth and forever the Bloom Garden will belong to the pupils of Shadow Academy.' Then, looking around, Madam de Scrazziola

136

asked, 'Where is Lottie Luna? Because I believe that, without her, this garden would never have existed.'

'I'm here.' Lottie, blushing furiously, stepped forward.

Madam de Scrazziola gave her a formal little bow and held out the scroll. 'Lottie Luna, please accept the ownership of the Bloom Garden on behalf of all your fellow pupils.'

'Three cheers for Lottie Luna!' shouted Wilf,

and the cheers echoed up to the evening sky.

Jaws, watching from the branch of a cherry tree, saw Lottie's moonstone necklace was shining as bright as the stars up above, and he sighed happily.

'Thank you so much, Madam de Scrazziola,' Lottie said, 'but I couldn't have done it without my friends – and all the other pupils.'

'Well said, Lottie!' Madam Grubeloff beamed at her. 'And now let us celebrate our glorious Bloom Garden with the most wonderful Evening Howl ever!' She paused for a moment, and all the pupils and teachers fell silent.

'The time has come to join together,' she began. 'Everyone, take your neighbour's hand . . .'

The velvet indigo sky was patterned with clouds, but, as the Howl began, they floated

139

gently away and the moon turned everything to silver. Lottie, holding hands with Marjory and Wilf, looked up in wonder. 'It's a full moon!'

she whispered. 'How perfect is that?' She sighed happily. 'Aren't I just *so* lucky to be here . . . and tomorrow will be another glorious day!'

LOOK OUT FOR LOTTIE'S
NEXT ADVENTURE!

She isn't your average werewolf...

LOTTIE LUNA
AND THE TWILIGHT PARTY

VIVIAN FRENCH
Illustrated by Nathan Reed